Unicorn School

The Treasure Hunt

At last, all the teams had their maps and
bags and were ready to start.
The Tricorn raised his head so that his
horn sparkled in the sunlight. "Let the
treasure hunt begin!"

Linda Chapman lives in Leicestershire, England, with her family and two Bernese mountain dogs. She used to be a stage manager in the theater. When she is not writing, she spends her time looking after her two young daughters, horseback riding, and teaching drama.

Books by Linda Chapman

MY SECRET UNICORN series

UNICORN SCHOOL series

FIRST-CLASS FRIENDS

THE SURPRISE PARTY

THE TREASURE HUNT

The Treasure Hunt

Linda Chapman

Illustrated by Ann Kronheimer

SCHOLASTIC INC.

New York   Toronto   London   Auckland   Sydney
Mexico City   New Delhi   Hong Kong   Buenos Aires

ISBN-13: 978-0-545-05365-5
ISBN-10: 0-545-05365-X

12 11 10 9 8 7 6 5 4 3   11 12 13/0

Printed in the U.S.A.
First printing, December 2008

To Luca Misra, who is a real treasure

Contents

Chapter One

Exciting News!

"Oh, wow!" Willow stared at the new poster on the school bulletin board. The title was written in large purple letters:

WINTER TREASURE HUNT!

Willow read quickly:

A treasure hunt will take place this Saturday, starting at 10 A.M.
All unicorns in the school may take part, but they must be in teams of four.
The clues will be hidden around Arcadia by the teachers.
Each team will have six clues to solve that will lead them to six objects.
The first team back with all their objects will win a term's supply of shamrock!
All teams wishing to take part must register with the chief elf by Friday.

Willow snorted in excitement. A treasure hunt! She couldn't wait to tell her best friends, Sapphire, Storm, and Troy. She was sure they would want to enter. *We can be a team together*, she thought. *It'll be such fun!*

She set off across the Assembly Fields toward Moonlight Meadows, where she had last seen her friends.

Willow and her friends were in Year One at Unicorn School. All the unicorns who lived in Arcadia went to school when they were nine to learn how to use their magic powers. They stayed at school until they were fifteen, and when they left, the smartest and bravest unicorns were chosen to be the Guardians of Arcadia. It was the job of the Guardians to look after all the other creatures who lived there.

Willow loved being at Unicorn

School and she really hoped she would be a Guardian one day!

She cantered into Moonlight Meadows, where all the unicorns ate and where they usually hung out between classes. The elves who worked at the school were clearing away lunch from four long tables. Unicorns were chatting, playing tag, grazing by the stream, and flying through the air. Willow spotted her three friends near one of the oak trees.

"Hi, Willow!" said Sapphire as Willow cantered over. "Where have you been?"

"Looking at the bulletin board. You'll never guess what!" Willow exclaimed.

"What?" Troy asked curiously. He was a very sporty-looking unicorn with a noble face and a long golden horn.

"There's going to be a treasure hunt!" Willow's eyes sparkled. "Isn't that cool? It's on Saturday, for teams of four."

"We can be a team!" said Storm. He was very big for his age but was very gentle and kind. "We can all go on it together."

"I've heard about the school having treasure hunts," said Troy. "They organize them to help us learn about the different parts of Arcadia."

"Did the poster say what the prize is?" Storm asked Willow.

"A term's supply of shamrock!" Willow declared.

Her friends all whinnied excitedly. Shamrock was their favorite food. It had magic in its leaves and tasted sweet and tingly.

"I hope we win!" said Storm.

"Me, too, but even if we don't, it should be fun just taking part," Sapphire said.

Storm and Willow nodded, but Troy shook his head. "I don't want to just take part. I want to win!"

Willow grinned at him. "You want to win everything, Troy!"

"That's because winning's fun," said Troy. "We'd better start practicing."

"Practising?" Storm echoed.

"How *can* you practice for a treasure hunt?" Sapphire asked in surprise.

"Well, we can practice flying and galloping as fast as we can," said Troy. "And we can study old treasure hunt maps and practice solving the clues on them. And learn the maps of Arcadia. There's lots of stuff we can do."

It sounded like a lot of work to Willow.

Just then, one of the elves blew a note on a large shell.

"We'd better go," Sapphire said, "or we'll be late for class."

Willow followed the others across the meadows, excitement buzzing through her. This treasure hunt was going to be fun!

Chapter
Two

The Healing Lesson

"Good afternoon, class," Sirona, the healing teacher, said as all the Year One unicorns gathered around her at the start of the lesson. "Today I am going to tell you about some of the magical creatures in Arcadia who you may one day need to heal if you become a Guardian,

Then you will practice your healing skills by using some plants."

Healing was one of Willow's favorite subjects at school. But as Sirona talked about the different magical creatures who lived in Arcadia, Willow found herself daydreaming about the treasure hunt. How many other teams would enter? How difficult would the clues be? Where in Arcadia would they be sent? Willow hadn't been to many places in Arcadia. She only really knew the meadows and woods where her parents lived and the school grounds. It would be so much fun to go exploring!

Suddenly, she was aware that

Sirona had just asked the class a question about kelpies, a type of pixielike creature that lived in streams.

I'd better concentrate, Willow thought guiltily as she realized she couldn't answer the question because she hadn't been listening to what Sirona had been saying. But it was hard when the thoughts of the treasure hunt were whirling around in her brain, and Willow was glad when Sirona stopped talking and they actually got to do some healing magic themselves.

Sirona gave them each a wilted plant. The flower head and leaves on each plant were all floppy.

"I would like you to try to heal the plant I have given you," Sirona said. "Concentrate on feeling well and healthy. Let that feeling grow in your mind, and then touch the plant with your horn. Your horn will start to glow if the magic is working. If your magic is strong enough, the plant will be healed."

Willow looked at her plant. Its orange flower was drooping sadly. *I can do this*, she thought confidently. She was good at healing. She shut her eyes and thought about feeling healthy. She let the feeling build and grow, and when it felt as if it was about to burst out of her, she opened her eyes and touched her horn to the orange flower. Sparks seemed to shoot through her. Her horn glowed a brilliant silver, and she felt magic flowing from her and into the flower. To her delight, the flower began to move upward toward the sky and its stalk stiffened. Willow took her horn away. The flower was healed!

"Good job, Willow!" Sirona exclaimed.

Willow looked around the class. Although some of the others had managed to make their flowers look a bit healthier, no one else had managed to heal their plant the way she had. Sirona smiled. "You have a natural talent for healing, Willow. Maybe you'll be a Guardian of Arcadia one day."

Willow glowed. Sirona couldn't have said anything to make her happier. "I'd love to be!" she said.

After the class had finished, Storm, Sapphire, and Troy joined Willow as they headed back to Moonlight Meadows.

"You healed your plant really well," Storm said to Willow.

"Thanks." Willow smiled.

"I wish I was as good as you," said Sapphire enviously. "I'm useless at healing. My plant didn't get better at all."

"You're lots better than me at rose-quartz gazing, though," Willow told her. "You always manage to see things in the rose quartz. I usually just get a blur."

When unicorns touched their horns to rocks of rose quartz, they were supposed to be able to use their magic to try to see what was happening in other parts of Arcadia. But it was tricky to do.

"We're all good at different things," said Storm. "I really liked it when Sirona was telling us about the other magical creatures in Arcadia. I never knew that dragons sometimes lose their puff, or that kelpies can catch colds."

Sapphire nodded. "It was really interesting."

Willow began to wish she'd listened harder at the beginning of the lesson. "What was Sirona saying?" she asked.

Troy snorted. "How can you three talk about boring lessons when we've got the treasure hunt to think about? After supper tonight let's go to the library and look up old treasure hunt maps and practice solving the clues. Then, tomorrow morning, why don't we meet early and practice flying?"

Willow exchanged looks with the other two.

"Do we really need to?" Storm asked.

"Yes," Troy said bossily. "We do.

We'll meet at the library at six o'clock. Okay?"

They nodded slowly. "Okay," they all said.

Troy stamped his hoof. "When we win the treasure hunt you'll thank me. Just wait and see!"

Troy, Willow, Storm, and Sapphire met at the library at six o'clock as planned.

"The maps and clues for the old treasure hunts are kept over here," Troy whispered, leading the way to the back of the big room. "I spoke to the librarian earlier, and she said it was fine for us to look at them. The clues will all be different on this year's hunt, so it's not cheating, it's just practicing."

He pulled a dark leather book off the shelf with his mouth and put it down on a nearby table. They all crowded around. Inside there were ten maps of Arcadia, each with six clues to different places and a set of answers.

"Look at all these names," Willow said. There were so many places marked on the map! She read some of them out: "Dragon's Peak, Mermaid Beach, Butterfly Hollow, Cockatrice Cavern, Lion Forest, Echo Cove, Phoenix Mountain." She looked at the others. "Oh, wow, I can't *wait* to go exploring!"

"Let's read the clues and see if we can figure them out," Troy said. "Here's the first one. It's supposed to help you find a place on the map." He read out: "'*I have a floor but no walls or a door. I make no noise but I sound like I roar.*'"

Sapphire looked blank. "What does that mean?"

"I don't know," said Willow. "What's got a floor but no walls or a door?"

"A forest!" said Storm. "It's an easy clue. I bet it means go to Lion Forest. A forest has a floor but no walls or a door, and it doesn't make any noise but its name makes it sound as if it roars."

"You're right!" said Troy, checking the answers.

"Let's try another one," said Willow. She read out: "'*Scales aplenty and snorting flame, follow me to play the game.*'"

Once again Storm got the answer really quickly. "I think it means go to Dragon's Peak, because dragons breathe fire and have scales."

Sapphire checked the list of answers. "You're right again. You're really good at this, Storm."

"I like solving problems," Storm said happily.

"This is wonderful!" said Troy, looking delighted. "We'll have a great chance of winning with you answering all the clues, Storm."

They practiced solving more clues, and then Troy spread all the maps out on the table. "Now, let's try to memorize these," he said. "They've all got different parts of Arcadia labeled on them. If we learn them all, we'll know where the places are, and when we get our clues on Saturday we won't have to spend ages looking over the map and trying to decide how to get there."

"Do we have to? I'm tired now," Willow said.

"Me, too." Sapphire yawned.

Storm nodded. "We can look at the maps tomorrow, Troy."

"I want to look now!" Troy insisted.

Storm and Sapphire hesitated, but Willow shook her head firmly. "Count me out. I think it's silly. We don't need to learn the maps. We'll have a map with us."

"Fine," Troy said huffily. "You guys can go back to the stables, but I'm going to stay and learn the maps. I think it'll help us win."

Sapphire, Storm, and Willow left him in the library. "Troy's taking this treasure hunt really seriously, isn't he?" said Sapphire.

Willow nodded. "I wish he could see that it's going to be fun whether we win or not."

"Do you think he *will* try to make us get up early to practice flying?" Storm said.

"I hope not," said Sapphire. She didn't like getting up early.

Willow grinned. "I bet he will!"

Flying Through Snow!

"Wake up, wake up!" Willow blinked her eyes open the next morning. Troy was standing next to her in the stall. He poked her with his horn. "Come on! We're going to practice flying, Willow!" He bounced out of her stall. "Time to wake up, Sapphire!

Come on, Storm!"

Willow yawned and got slowly to her feet. It was *very* early in the morning.

"Do we *have* to get up now?" she heard Sapphire complain.

"Yes!" Troy said. "The more practice we get the better, and it's a lovely morning for flying!"

They all left the cloud stable and went outside. Troy was certainly right about it being a lovely morning. The sun was shining, although it was very cold. The grass in Moonlight Meadows was covered with frost, and their breath froze in the air.

"Come on, come on!" Troy said bossily as soon as they reached the

Flying Heath. "Line up and let's practice racing starts."

"But why?" Willow asked. "We're not having a race. We're going on a treasure hunt!"

"Yes, but every second might count," said Troy.

Willow opened her mouth to argue, but Sapphire nudged her. "Just do what he says," she said in a low voice. "Otherwise, we'll never get back in time for breakfast!"

Willow knew Sapphire was right, so she didn't say anything but lined up with the others.

"On your mark. Get set. Go!" Troy shouted.

They all took off. Troy was easily

the quickest, but he always was. He was one of the fastest unicorns in the whole school, even though he was only a Year One.

"Come on, you can do better than that!" he said to the rest of them. "Try again! Storm, you have to push off betterer — push down with both of your back legs. Sapphire, you took off okay, but then you slowed down — you have to keep going. And Willow, you didn't look as if

you were trying at all. Let's try
again."

They lined up. Storm looked
flustered. He tried too hard to push
off with his back legs and ended up
shooting straight into the air and
losing control. Sapphire was
concentrating so hard on trying to
fly fast after she'd taken off that she
didn't see him.

"Ow!" they both gasped as they
banged into each other. They
weren't hurt, and they both started
to laugh.

Willow giggled, too, and landed. "I
don't think your training's doing us
much good," she said teasingly to Troy.

He glared at her and then at the

others. "You're not taking this seriously enough. Come on. Let's try again!"

Willow was very relieved when the horn blew for breakfast. "I'm glad the treasure hunt's tomorrow," she muttered to Sapphire. "Imagine if it was weeks away and Troy made us do this *every* morning."

Sapphire shuddered at the thought. "He is being a little annoying."

"A little?" said Willow. "A lot! I wish he didn't want to win so much."

They trotted thankfully to the table. There were buckets full of a warm bran mash mixed with carrots and apples all along the table.

"Yum!" said Willow, plunging her head into a bucket. It was her favorite breakfast on a cold day!

As she finished the last mouthful she felt something soft and cold land on her head. She looked up. "Snow!" She gasped as she saw flakes of snow floating down from the sky. "It's snowing!"

The other unicorns whinnied in excitement.

"Oh, wow!" said Troy. "We'll get to fly through it during our flying lesson after breakfast."

"And at lunchtime we can make a snow unicorn," said Sapphire. "I hope it falls really thickly!"

★

After breakfast, they headed off to the Flying Heath for their first class of the day. Atlas, their flying teacher, was waiting for them. "We were going to practice turning and changing direction today," he told them. "But I think we'll practice flying through snow instead. Has anyone used their magic to fly through snow before?"

The Year Ones all shook their heads. Unicorns didn't usually do much magic before they started school, and it was the first time it had snowed since they had begun there.

"Well, I think you're really going to enjoy it," Atlas told them.

Storm raised his horn. "Isn't it hard to fly through snow?"

"Yes," put in Flint, another Year One unicorn. "It must be really hard to see."

"It would be, but we have a special type of magic we can use to help us," said Atlas. "To make it work, you must imagine feeling as warm as you can. Let the feeling flow out through your horn, and see what happens. Off you go!"

The unicorns rose into the sky.

Feel warm, feel warm, Willow thought to herself. She imagined feeling toasty and snug in her cloud stall. The sensation rose inside her, but the next minute she found herself swerving out of control and heading straight toward the ground. She whizzed upward just in time. It was really hard to concentrate on flying and to think about feeling warm at the same time!

Looking around, she was relieved to see that she wasn't the only one having difficulty doing both. All around her, unicorns were swerving and crashing into one another. But then she caught her breath. High above them all, Troy was flying through the snow. Purple stars streamed from the tip of his horn. They flowed together into an arch over his back, casting a glow all around him. As the snowflakes fell

on the arch, they melted. Troy flew
through the snow in a bubble of
magic lilac light.

Willow caught her breath and for
a moment forgot how annoyed she
was with Troy for being so bossy
about the treasure hunt. He really
was wonderful at anything to do

with flying. "Well done!" she shouted, cantering up into the air.

He grinned at her as she joined him. "Thanks, Willow! This is cool!"

"I can't do it at all," said Willow, shaking her head as the flakes blinded her. "I'm going to have to go back down."

"No, wait," said Troy. "Here, fly with me under my light, and then see if you can make the magic work, too."

"Okay," said Willow eagerly. She reached his side, and cantering along in time with him through the air, she found that his magic light kept the snowflakes off her, too.

She tried to imagine a feeling of warmth again. But as she concentrated on it she felt herself starting to worry that she was going to crash, so she quickly stopped.

"Don't worry," Troy told her, nudging her neck with his nose. "I'll make sure you don't fly into anything. Try again."

Willow flew even closer to him so their sides were touching, and then she concentrated again. This time the feeling of warmth flooded through her and out of her horn. Suddenly, purple stars of her own started to appear. "I'm doing it!" she exclaimed as a rainbow of light formed over her body.

"You *are* doing it!" said Troy. "Now you can concentrate on flying, too." He edged away. "See, you're on your own!"

Willow realized she was. She whinnied in delight. Together they cantered and swooped through the snowy sky.

"Well done!" Atlas cried, coming over to them. "It normally takes a lot of practice to be able to fly through snow."

"It was Troy!" said Willow gratefully. "He helped me. I couldn't have done it without him!"

Troy looked very pleased. "You did it yourself, really. I just gave you a little help."

"Well, it's really great to see you working as a team," said Atlas. "Off you go!"

Willow and Troy flew into the sky. "Now that you know how to do it, let's go and help the others," said Troy, looking over to where Storm and Sapphire were trying to fly through the snow but failing. "I'll help Storm learn, and you can help Sapphire."

"Okay," said Willow, thrilled with her new skill. "Come on!"

Chapter Four

Troy's Treasure Hunters

By the end of the flying lesson, Sapphire and Storm were swooping and diving through the snow as easily as Willow and Troy. It was great just to be having fun together rather than arguing about the treasure hunt, but the peace didn't last for long. At lunchtime,

Troy remembered they had to practice and tried to get them all to go to the library to look at the maps again.

"But I want to make a snow unicorn," said Storm. "We don't know how long the snow will last."

"Yeah," agreed Willow. "We can look at boring maps another time!"

"The treasure hunt's tomorrow," Troy told them. "We should use all the time we have, and we also need to think of a name for our team. We have to register it by the end of today."

Sapphire sighed. "Okay, let's go to the library and do some treasure hunt stuff."

But Willow shook her head. She didn't want to spend all of her lunchtime in the library. "No, I'm not going," she decided. "I'm going to make a snow unicorn!"

"Willow!" Troy said crossly. "Don't you care about this treasure hunt at all?"

"Of course I do. I just don't see why we need to waste our time learning maps," Willow argued. "It won't help!"

"Yes it will! You're being stupid!" Troy told her.

"And you're just being annoying!" she snapped angrily.

"Stop it, you two!" Sapphire broke in.

Willow and Troy shut up.

"Don't argue," said Sapphire, stepping forward. "Please!"

Troy looked at her. "You'll come and learn the maps with me, won't you, Sapphire?" he said pleadingly.

"Well . . ." Sapphire looked torn. "Oh, okay, then," she sighed.

"Storm, you'll come and make a snow unicorn with me, won't you?" Willow said quickly.

Storm looked unhappy. "Can't we do something together?" he said.

But Troy was already trotting away with a reluctant Sapphire.

"It looks like we can't," Willow told Storm. "Or at least not while Troy's being so crazy about winning this treasure hunt. Oh, well." She tried to be cheerful. "I bet we'll have a much better time than they will!"

But it wasn't nearly as much fun making a snow unicorn on their own.

"There!" Willow said brightly, stepping back after a while. "It looks great."

Storm looked at it. "I suppose. But we'd have been able to make a much bigger one if Troy and Sapphire had helped us. And it *would* have been more fun. It's always better when we do things together — like when you and Troy helped Sapphire and me learn to fly through snow earlier. That was wonderful."

Willow sighed. She was still feeling angry with Troy, but she knew Storm was right. It *was* more fun when they did things together.

Just then Sapphire came back. "Hey! That looks great!" she said, looking at their snow unicorn. "Can I help finish it?"

"Of course," Willow told her. "Where's Troy?"

"I don't know. He said he had to

do something for the treasure hunt, and he left." Sapphire looked at the snow unicorn. "I wish we could have helped you make the unicorn. I like it much more when we do stuff all together," she said wistfully.

"So you didn't have lots of fun in the library, then?" Willow asked.

"No." Sapphire looked guilty and giggled. "Don't tell Troy this, but it was really boring!"

Storm nuzzled her. "Well, we missed you. Come on, let's finish this snow unicorn."

They were just finishing by putting in stones for the snow unicorn's eyes when Troy came cantering into the meadows. Willow noticed that he was looking very pleased with himself. "All done!" he announced.

"What's all done?" Willow asked, curious.

"I've registered our team for the treasure hunt," said Troy.

"You've registered us?" said Storm

in surprise. "But that means you must have chosen a name."

Troy shook his mane back. "Yep! I've called us . . ." He paused, looking very proud. "Troy's Treasure Hunters!"

They all stared at him.

"Troy's Treasure Hunters!" Willow echoed.

Troy nodded. "It's a cool name, isn't it?"

"Um . . ." Sapphire began slowly.

"No!" Willow broke in. "It's not a cool name at all! It makes us sound like we're your team! You shouldn't have registered without talking to the rest of us, Troy!"

"Well, none of the rest of you seemed that interested in this treasure hunt." Troy looked angry. "I think you should be grateful to me."

"We are," Sapphire said hastily. "It's fine, Troy. Thank you for registering us."

Troy stamped huffily. "I'll see you later!" He cantered off.

Willow swung around to the others. "I can't believe he registered the team's name without talking to us about it!"

"I wish he hadn't," said Storm. "But he didn't mean to upset us, Willow."

"No, I'm sure he didn't," said Sapphire.

"Huh!" Willow snorted. She looked in the direction Troy had gone. "I'm going to be glad when the treasure hunt's over. I almost wish it wasn't happening!"

Sapphire nuzzled her. "Don't be like that. You know it will be fun. Troy's just being his usual bossy self. Try to ignore him and just have a good time. That's what I'm going to do."

Willow looked at her and felt a rush of affection. Sapphire was so sensible. And she was right. There really was no point getting upset about Troy wanting to win so much and being so bossy. That was just the way he was. "Okay," she said, nuzzling Sapphire back. "It'll still be fun even if Troy is being his bossiest ever." She took a deep breath. "I promise I'll try really hard not to get mad at him tomorrow. I'll just enjoy myself!"

Sapphire whinnied. "Cool!"

Storm nodded. "We're all going to have a great time. I know we are!"

The Treasure Hunt

When Willow woke up the
following day she looked out
the window. More snow had fallen
in the night, and the sun was
shining in a clear blue sky.

Excitement fizzed through her. It
was the day of the treasure hunt,
and even the thought of Troy being

bossy all day couldn't dampen her happiness.

She could hear the others around her getting up. The other unicorns who shared their stable — Topaz, Starlight, Flint, and Ash — were also entering the treasure hunt as a team.

"See you down there," Topaz called as Willow left the stable.

"Yeah, good luck today," Willow told her.

Topaz smiled. "You, too!"

"What are you doing, wishing the other team good luck, Willow?" Troy said angrily as he joined her on the way to breakfast.

Willow felt a flicker of annoyance, but she squashed it down. "I was just trying to be friendly," she replied.

Troy opened his mouth, but Willow trotted away before he could say anything else that would annoy her. "Come on. I'm hungry!"

They ate their breakfast as fast as they could. Everyone was talking about the treasure hunt. Nearly everyone in the school was going to be taking part.

"I had another look at the maps yesterday evening," Troy hissed to Willow, Sapphire, and Storm. "I think I know them by heart now. I should be able to find the way to any of the places we have to go to."

"Wouldn't it be amazing if we

won the shamrock?" Sapphire said.

"A whole term's supply!" said
Storm. "Where are the teachers
keeping it?"

"In one of the feed rooms near
the kitchens," said Troy, who seemed
to know everything there was to
know about the treasure hunt. "One
of the elves told me that if
shamrock gets too cold it spoils and
can't be eaten. They're going to
bring it out in boxes at the start of
the treasure hunt." He looked
around. "Let's go to the Assembly
Fields now that we've finished
breakfast. That's where the teachers
will be giving out the maps. Maybe
we can get ours early and start

working on what the first clue means!"

But although Willow's team was one of the first on to the Assembly Fields, Atlas wouldn't let them have their treasure map. "No one is going to get a map until the treasure hunt officially starts," the flying teacher told them. "The Tricorn is going to talk to everyone taking part, and then we'll give out the maps so you all get them at the same time."

By a quarter to ten, the Assembly Fields were full of excited unicorns. They all fell silent as the Tricorn — the school's headmaster — walked into the field. He was a very noble-looking unicorn with a horn of three colors — bronze, silver, and gold — and he was accompanied by a team of elves carrying wooden boxes that they placed in front of the platform.

The Tricorn stepped onto the platform and looked around at the unicorns. As the last box was put down, he began to speak. "Good morning, everyone. I'm glad to see so many of you taking part in the annual winter treasure hunt this year. As you know, you have to try to find six objects. This year, they will be six crystals, all labeled with a team's name. To find the crystals, you must follow the clues. The first team back with all six of their crystals will win the prize." He nodded toward the wooden crates and smiled. "A term's supply of shamrock. Fly swiftly, solve your clues wisely, and the prize might be yours. Only one team can win, but I hope that you will all gain something from visiting the different places in Arcadia as you collect your objects. Good luck, teams! The teachers will now give out the treasure maps. Please do not turn them over until the chief elf blows his horn."

The teachers trotted among the teams, giving out the maps. They also gave each team a leather bag to put their crystals into.

"I'll wear it," said Troy quickly. He took the bag from Atlas and slipped it over his head.

Willow frowned, but she was still determined she wasn't going to get angry with Troy. She didn't want *anything* to ruin the day.

At last, all the teams had their maps and bags and were ready to start.

The Tricorn raised his head so that his horn sparkled in the sunlight. "Let the treasure hunt begin!"

The chief elf blew a long note, and all the teams turned their maps over. Willow noticed that not all the parts of Arcadia were named, just some of them.

"What does the first clue say?" Storm asked eagerly.

The clue to the first place they had to go to was written at the top of the map.

"Clue one," Troy read. "'*A very pretty thing am I, you'll see me in the pale-blue sky. Delicate, fragile on the wing, indeed I am a pretty thing. What am I?*'"

They all looked at each other.

Willow reread the clue. "A pretty thing? On the wing? What does it mean?"

"We have to be quick!" Troy urged, glancing around. "Some of the other teams are setting off already."

"Maybe it's talking about a bird," Sapphire suggested. "Look, there is a place on the map called Bird's View. It could mean we have to go there."

"Great! Let's go!" said Troy, taking off.

"No, Troy! Wait!" exclaimed Storm. "It's not a bird. A bird's a good guess, Sapphire, but they're not really delicate and fragile, are they? I think it's a butterfly!"

"Which means we probably need to go to Butterfly Hollow!" said Willow. "I bet you're right, Storm."

"I know how to get there," said Troy. "Come on!"

They took off after him. They flew above the Assembly Fields and out across the courtyard. The air was filled with unicorns flying in different directions as they followed their clues.

"Wait, Troy!" Willow called as Troy raced ahead.

"We can't keep up!" Sapphire whinnied to him.

But Troy didn't stop.

"Troy!" shouted Willow as she galloped through the sky. "We don't know the way to Butterfly Hollow." But he was too far off to hear. He flew into the distance.

"It's okay. I still have the map," said Storm. "Let's land and take a look at it and see if we can figure out where to go."

"Troy should have waited!" said Willow as they landed and Storm shook out the map. "He knows we can't fly as fast as he can!"

"Don't worry. It's not far away," said Sapphire. "Look, we just have to fly over that line of trees, and we'll be there."

They raced into the sky again. They were all out of breath when they finally reached Butterfly Hollow.

Troy was standing on a grassy hill, surrounded by white and yellow butterflies. He had a bright blue crystal with a piece of paper attached to it in his mouth. "What took you so long?" he asked, dropping the crystal onto the grass.

"You know we can't fly as fast as you!" Willow said. "You should have waited, Troy. We didn't know where we were going, so we had to look at the map. What's the point of you knowing all the places if you fly off and we still have to keep looking at the map to find where you've gone?"

Troy looked taken aback. "Oh." It was obvious he hadn't thought about that. "I guess I should have waited. Sorry." He looked at the crystal at his hooves and pricked his ears. "Well, at least you're here now, and I've found the second clue, so we can move on and solve it. Listen. "'*You heard me before and yet hear me again. Then I go until you call me again,*'" he read. "It's a really tricky one."

"No, it isn't!" said Storm. "The answer to the clue is an echo! You hear echoes again and again, and then they go away until you make another noise, or, as the clue says, 'call me again.' Look," he put the map down and pointed with his horn. "There's a place called Echo Cove. I bet that's where we have to go!"

"Cool!" exclaimed Troy. "Let's go!"

"Wait!" called Willow. But even though Troy did slow down and wait for them this time, he couldn't resist speeding up as they drew near Echo Cove, a small, sandy beach by the sea.

By the time the other three had landed, Troy had already discovered their next clue. It was attached to an emerald green crystal that he had found half buried in the sand. "I've got it! I've got it!" he whinnied in delight.

Willow sighed. It was great that Troy knew Arcadia so well, because it meant they didn't have to spend ages studying the map. But by using his knowledge to race on ahead, Troy was taking the fun out of the treasure hunt for the rest of them.

"It would have been more fun if we'd all looked for the crystal together," said Sapphire.

"Don't be silly. We have to find them as quickly as possible," said Troy. "That's the point."

"Well, actually . . ." Willow began to argue. But before she could say any more, Troy was shushing her.

"Be quiet, Willow," he interrupted bossily. "We have to solve the next clue. It's in two parts."

Willow almost exploded with the effort of keeping her temper. Didn't Troy realize how annoying he was being? Troy read the clue out loud. "'*I can run but never walk. I have a mouth but never talk. I have a bed but never sleep. I have a head but never weep.*'" That's the first part, and the second says, '*A quiet noise is in my* name. *Find me quick, and play the game!*"

"The first part's easy," said Storm. "It's talking about a river. Water runs in a river, and the end of the river is called the mouth, and the head of the river is where it starts. So we need to find a river."

"But which one? There are lots in Arcadia," said Troy.

"It sounds like the name of the river has something to do with a quiet noise," said Willow. "Let's look at the map." She picked it up with her mouth.

"Here, let me look!" said Troy, trying to take it from her.

"No, I want to see," said Willow, holding on tight.

"Let me look!" repeated Troy.

"No!" Willow exclaimed. Her voice was muffled by the map in her mouth, and she was feeling more and more angry with Troy. "We're supposed to be a team, Troy! You can't do everything on your own. It's not fair! Let *me* look this time!"

"No!" Troy yanked at the map with his teeth. There was a loud ripping sound.

Willow and Troy stared at each other. They each had half the map in their mouths. It had been torn in two!

Chapter
Six

The Noise in the Trees

"Oh, no!" Storm exclaimed. "It wasn't me!" both Willow and Troy said immediately.

"It *was* you!" Willow whinnied furiously at Troy. "You should have let me see!"

"You shouldn't have tried to hang

on to it!" said Troy. "You're the one who ripped it!"

"No, I didn't!"

"Stop arguing, you two!" Sapphire whinnied.

"Yes! It was both your faults," said Storm. "You shouldn't have been quarreling over the map. Now it's ripped, and we're not even going to be able to finish the treasure hunt, let alone win it! Just look at it!"

The map had a big jagged tear down the middle.

"If we put the two halves back together we might be able to read it," said Sapphire hopefully as Willow and Troy glared at each other. "Let's try."

They carefully placed the two halves of the map next to each other. It was hard to read the writing where the rip was, but Willow could just make out some words that labeled a river on the map. "The Whispering River," she said.

"That must be where the next clue is!" said Sapphire. "It's a river and whispering is a quiet noise!"

"Let's go!" said Troy.

They flew there side by side. Willow didn't say a word to Troy. She was feeling so mad at him, she knew that if she spoke they'd end up arguing. She didn't want to upset Sapphire and Storm.

At last, they reached the river. It glittered in the sunlight, stretching up toward the mountains in one direction and down to the sea in another. All around it the land was covered with snow. "I wonder where the crystal is," said Sapphire.

"Let's separate and each search a different place," Troy said. "I'll go up to where it starts in the mountains. Sapphire, you search the next part. Willow, you search around here, and

Storm, you search nearer the sea."

They all nodded. It looked like this clue was going to be really tough to find!

Willow began to search along the riverbank. After a little way, the river entered some trees whose branches were bending down, heavy with snow. Willow trotted between the trees, her eyes scanning the ground, looking for a bright crystal with a message attached.

Suddenly, she heard a noise. It was a snuffling, snorting kind of noise. She stopped. It was coming from a nearby cluster of oak trees. It sounded like a creature, but what kind of creature made a noise like that?

Willow hesitated, but then curiosity got the better of her and she walked over to the oak trees. Peering around the first one, she gasped! There, sitting on the ground, was a green baby dragon! It had two wings folded on its back, golden scales on its tummy, and big dark eyes with long eyelashes.

It heard Willow gasp and jumped.

For a moment the baby dragon and Willow stared at each other.

"H–hello," Willow said uncertainly. She'd never met a dragon before. They were very rare, and her parents had told her they usually lived in the mountains.

"Hello." The dragon had a husky voice. It sounded almost as though it had been crying. "Who . . . who are you?"

"I'm Willow," Willow replied. "What's your name?"

"Littleclaw," said the dragon.

"Are you okay?" Willow asked him, stepping closer. Littleclaw was shivering.

The baby dragon shook his head. "I'm cold and lost," he said. "I've just learned to fly. My parents told me not to go too far, but when I started flying down the mountain, it was such fun that I kept going. I went on and on and then landed here, and now I can't seem to fly anymore."

He looked hopefully at Willow. "Can you help me? My mom and dad have told me stories about how unicorns look after the other creatures in Arcadia. Can you help me get home?"

Willow stared at him. "I'd love to, but I'm not a grown-up unicorn. I'm still in school." She looked at the shivering dragon. Her heart went out to him. "But maybe I can help. Let me get my friends. Wait here a minute!"

"Okay," said Littleclaw. "But you will come back soon, won't you?"

"I promise!" said Willow.

Willow raced to find Storm, Sapphire, and Troy. They were astonished to hear about the dragon. Ten minutes later they were all standing in the clearing, staring at Littleclaw.

"So you really can't find your way home?" Sapphire said.

"No. After I landed by the river, I found I couldn't take off again," Littleclaw told her anxiously. "I don't know why."

Troy turned impatiently to the others. "We're wasting time. His parents will come looking for him, and he'll be fine. We need to move on and find our next clue."

"Troy!" Willow said, shocked. "We can't just leave him!"

"But we'll lose the treasure hunt if we help him!" Troy protested.

"That doesn't matter," Sapphire said hotly. "We're supposed to be the Guardians of Arcadia, Troy. Littleclaw needs our help!"

"Sapphire and Willow are right," agreed Storm. "The treasure hunt doesn't matter." He breathed softly on the little dragon to try to warm him up. "Don't worry, we'll help you find your way back home."

The dragon looked at him gratefully. "Thank you."

For a moment, Troy looked torn, but then a stubborn look crossed his face. He shook his head. "Let's finish the treasure hunt, get back to school, and then we can tell the teachers about Littleclaw. They can help him if his parents haven't found him by then."

"Oh, please don't leave me," Littleclaw said anxiously.

Willow looked at him. "Don't worry, we won't." She glared at Troy. "You can go on with the treasure hunt if you want, Troy. We're going to help Littleclaw."

"Fine," Troy said angrily. "If you're going to be like that, I'll finish the treasure hunt on my own!"

And he turned and cantered out of the trees.

Chapter Seven

Lost!

"**I** can't believe Troy's gone!" said Willow.

"Me, neither," said Sapphire, looking shocked. "I know winning the treasure hunt's important to him, but I never thought he'd go off like that. Not when Littleclaw needs our help."

"Let's try to forget about it for now," said Storm. "We need to concentrate on helping Littleclaw get home." He looked at the baby dragon. "Why can't you fly?"

"I don't know, but whenever I try, nothing happens," replied Littleclaw.

"Let's see," suggested Willow.

They all watched as Littleclaw stretched out his wings. "Okay."

He blew hard and leaped upward. He beat his green wings, and his legs scrabbled in the air, but he didn't fly. He just flopped back to the ground and landed with a thump. "See?"

Storm frowned thoughtfully. "Let's think about this. You're doing

everything you normally do?"
Littleclaw nodded.

"I thought dragons had to let out
a puff of smoke before they flew,"
Sapphire said. "That's what we were
told in our healing class."

"We do,' said Littleclaw.

"But you didn't do that," Willow
told him.

"Didn't I?" Littleclaw looked

surprised. "I thought I did. Look."
He blew hard, but not even a wisp
of smoke left his nostrils. "Oh," he
said in alarm.

"I bet it's because you've gotten
too cold in the snow!" Storm
exclaimed. "Sirona told us about it
in healing. She said that when
dragons, particularly young ones, get
really cold, their fire goes out. They
need healing magic to get it working
again." He turned to Willow. "You're
the best of us all at healing, Willow.
Why don't you try healing
Littleclaw."

"Oh, yes, please do! Please!" the
little dragon said, bouncing up and
down in excitement.

Willow took a deep breath. "Okay," she said. "But I've never done anything like this before."

Sapphire looked at her. "Just believe you can do it," she said. "You know that's what we're always told is the most important thing when we do magic."

Willow looked at Littleclaw. Sapphire was right. *I can do it*, she thought. *I can heal him*. Shutting her eyes, she imagined a fire burning inside her. She felt her whole body tingle. She could feel the magic building and glowing. She opened her eyes and touched her horn to Littleclaw's chest. She saw her horn glow silver, heard the little dragon gasp, and felt magic spark through her and into him.

"I feel all warm!" Littleclaw cried.

Willow lifted her horn. "See if you can blow smoke now!"

Littleclaw breathed out in a whoosh. A puff of gray smoke shot out of his nostrils. "My fire's back!" he cried. He puffed again, stretched his wings, and the next minute he was rising off the ground. With one flap of his wings he soared upward toward the branches. "I can fly again! You've cured me, Willow!"

Willow, Sapphire, and Storm exchanged delighted looks. The baby dragon flew around the oak tree. "Whee!"

The unicorns all flew up to join him. Together they glided through the branches and into the sky. Littleclaw's wings beat hard.

"Now you can fly home," Sapphire told the little dragon. "Where do you live?"

Littleclaw looked around, and an uncertain frown crossed his face.

"I . . . er . . . I don't know."

"What do you mean, you don't know?" asked Willow.

"Well, I think it's called Dragon's Point or Dragon's Peak . . ." Littleclaw looked unsure. "I *think* it's Dragon's Peak. I know it's in the mountains, but I don't know which ones."

They all looked around. There were mountains to the north, the east, and the west.

"What are we going to do?" Willow asked the others.

"Maybe the map will help," suggested Sapphire.

"Yes, good idea," Willow agreed. "You stay here, Littleclaw," she said, not wanting the dragon to see they were feeling really worried. "And we'll look at the map." They landed and looked at the two halves of the map, but although the mountains were all marked, there was nothing to suggest where Dragon's Peak was. Willow's heart sank. She looked at Sapphire and Storm. "What are we going to do?"

Just then there was a soft cough behind them. They swung around. Troy was standing there.

"Troy!" Willow gasped.

Troy hung his head. "I — I'm sorry," he said. "I shouldn't have gone away like that. I got to the next clue and I realized I don't want to do the treasure hunt on my own. And I do want to help Littleclaw."

Sapphire trotted over and nuzzled him. "Oh, Troy."

"I wish I hadn't been so stupid," he said.

Willow felt a rush of relief. It had been horrible to think of Troy leaving without them. "You came back," she told him. "That's all that matters. Oh, Troy, I'm so glad you did."

"Me, too," he said. "How's Littleclaw?"

"Flying again," said Storm. "He'd lost his puff, but Willow healed him."

"Cool!" Troy said, looking admiringly at Willow.

"The only problem now is that he can't remember his way home. He thinks he lives in a place called Dragon's Peak," said Willow. "But he doesn't know where it is or how to get there."

Troy stamped a hoof. "I do."

"Really?" said Willow.

Troy nodded. "Dragon's Peak was marked on several of the old treasure maps I studied in the library. It's not marked on our map because none of our clues led us there, but I'm sure I can find it."

"What are we waiting for?" Willow said in delight. "Let's go!"

Chapter Eight

Dragon's Peak

Willow and her friends flew into the sky. Littleclaw was waiting for them, looking worried.

"It's all right, Littleclaw!" Willow called. "Troy's come back,. and he thinks he knows how to get you home to Dragon's Peak."

"It might be a good idea just to

be sure that's where you really do live and that your parents are there," said Sapphire, "rather than fly all the way there and find out it's not the right place."

"How can we do that?" asked Littleclaw.

"Rose quartz," said Sapphire. "I can use it to look at any place in Arcadia I want. There's some in the trees."

They all flew down, and Sapphire touched her horn to the rose quartz she had seen. "Dragon's Peak," she murmured.

There was a purple flash, and the rock glowed like a mirror. Smoke spread out over the surface. As it

cleared, Willow could see a picture
in the rock. It showed a mountain
with a summit covered in a pink
cloud. There was a cave in the
mountainside, and a large green
dragon was standing outside the
cave, calling out anxiously.

"That's my mom!" cried Littleclaw.

"So that *is* your home! You *do* live
on Dragon's Peak," said Sapphire.

"Let's go, then!" said Troy.

Sapphire took her horn away from
the rock, and the picture vanished.
The unicorns and Littleclaw rose
into the air. As they flew above the
trees, a few flakes of snow swirled
down.

Littleclaw shivered as the snow fell

on his wings. "I don't like flying in the snow. It's really cold!"

"Fly close to me," Willow told the little dragon. "We don't want to risk your fire going out again!" She thought warm thoughts, and the next second, purple stars were shooting out of her horn.

"Oh, wow!" Littleclaw gasped, looking up in wonder at the purple rainbow that arched over him and Willow, keeping the snow off them. "You're so clever! All of you! I'm really glad you're here to look after me."

Willow felt a glow of pride. It was great being able to help.

"Which way is it?" Sapphire called to Troy. They all had stars streaming out of their horns.

"Dragon's Peak is in the mountains to the west," he called. "Follow me!"

The others joined him.

Willow grinned at Troy. "You know, I never thought I'd say this, but I'm glad you wanted to win the treasure hunt so much. If you hadn't, you wouldn't have studied the maps, and we wouldn't have known which way to go now."

Troy smiled. "True, but I wish I hadn't been so silly earlier. I should have realized that helping Littleclaw was more important than winning."

"What made you come back?" Willow asked him.

"Well, I found the next clue, but it wasn't any fun, and as I was flying to the next place, I suddenly realized that I really wanted to be with all of you. I'd rather be helping Littleclaw than be on my own, even if it means not winning the treasure hunt."

Willow nudged him happily with her nose. "I'm so glad you came back!"

"Me, too." Troy snorted. "Anyway, even if I had continued, I wouldn't have won the treasure hunt. Storm's the one who's really good at solving clues. I'm lousy at it."

"We're all good at different things," Sapphire said. "You're great at finding your way to places, Troy. Storm's really good at solving puzzles. Willow, you're really good at healing, which helped Littleclaw get his puff back." She frowned. "I don't know what I'm good at."

"Making sure we don't argue too much!" Willow said. "And you're wonderful at rose-quartz gazing!"

"We make a great team when we work together," said Troy.

"The best!" said Storm.

They all whinnied happily and galloped on through the snowy sky.

When they reached their destination, Troy led the way to a jagged mountain with stony outcroppings that looked like dragon's teeth. There was a pink cloud above it just like the picture in the rose quartz.

"This is Dragon's Peak," said Troy.

"It is! It is!" cried Littleclaw,

blowing out a puff of smoke in excitement.

The pink cloud cast a glow over the whole mountain. It seemed to have an effect similar to the unicorns' purple rainbows — keeping everywhere warm. There wasn't a flake of snow on the mountainside, just green grass and a winding, clear stream.

Willow and the others let their purple rainbows disappear as they landed on the sloping side of the mountain.

"There's my cave!" cried Littleclaw. He bounded toward the entrance, his wings flapping. "Mom! Dad!"

There was a snort of relief, and

the large green dragon they'd seen in the rose quartz hurried to the cave entrance. "Littleclaw!" she exclaimed, her dark eyes widening in delight.

Littleclaw charged over. "Mom!" The big dragon folded her wings around him and hugged him tight. "Oh, Littleclaw, where have you been? We've been so worried about you! Your father's out looking for you."

"I flew too far and then lost my puff and couldn't fly." Littleclaw explained what had happened. His mother looked gratefully at Willow and the others.

"Thank you so much for bringing Littleclaw home," she said.

"That's okay!" said Willow happily. The dragon lifted her head and blew out three short smoke rings. They floated into the sky. "Your father will see the smoke and realize you're back," she said to Littleclaw.

He snuggled against her. "I'm sorry I got lost, Mom."

Willow glanced at her friends. They were all smiling. It felt wonderful to have brought

Littleclaw back safely. "We should go back to school now," said Willow.

"You must take something with you," said Littleclaw's mother. "To say thank you for finding Littleclaw. Here!" She turned her head and plucked a scale gently from her tail. It glinted and glimmered like an emerald as she held it out to them. It was beautiful. The unicorns stared at it in awe. None of them had ever seen a dragon's scale before.

"Thank you." Troy bowed and took it. He put it into the leather bag and then set off into the sky. "Bye, Littleclaw!"

"Bye!" Littleclaw called. "Thank you for helping me." He and his mom watched them go.

As the unicorns flew away from the Dragon's Peak they saw another big green dragon heading swiftly toward the cave.

"I bet that's Littleclaw's dad," said Willow happily. "I'm so glad we helped him!"

"Me, too!" said Sapphire. "Even if it means we've lost the treasure hunt."

Storm and Troy both whinnied in agreement.

"At least now we can just have fun finding the rest of our objects," said Willow. She shot forward. "Come on! We still have three left to find!'

Wish Magic

Willow, Storm, Sapphire, and Troy raced through Arcadia, finding their three remaining objects: a red crystal in an old tree trunk in Wilderness Wood, a yellow crystal hidden under a mossy bank in Moonflower Vale, and a pink crystal hidden in a sparkling rock pool on Mermaid Beach.

"We have them all," Willow said happily as Troy put the last crystal into the bag. "Now we can go back to school!"

As they flew back they joined a crowd of other unicorns also flying back to school, their bags bulging with crystals.

"I wonder which team won," said Sapphire as they flew through the school gates.

They flew to the platform where a group of unicorns was standing around the teachers and the Tricorn. "Who won?" Willow called out.

Oriel, a Year Three unicorn, looked up and whinnied. "My team did! We got back here ages ago. We're going to have all the shamrock!"

"Well done!" Troy said sportingly. He put down their bag on the table.

Atlas emptied it. As the dragon scale slid onto the tabletop, everyone gasped. "What's this?" Atlas exclaimed. He picked it up. It glinted and shone in the light.

"It's a dragon's scale." The Tricorn's deep voice broke the silence. He walked over and looked at the scale.

"How did you get this?" he asked curiously, looking at Willow, Storm, Troy, and Sapphire.

"We helped a baby dragon," Willow said. "He was lost." The story about Littleclaw poured out of her. All the other unicorns listened, spellbound. "We *had* to help him," Willow said to the Tricorn as she finished, hoping they weren't in trouble. "We couldn't just leave him."

The Tricorn smiled. "No, you did the right thing. You all acted as true future Guardians of Arcadia." Willow felt a rush of relief and pride. "And now you are lucky enough to have this." The Tricorn held up the scale.

"It's beautiful, isn't it?" said Sapphire happily.

"It's more than just beautiful, Sapphire," the Tricorn told her seriously. "Dragons' scales are immensely valuable. They are full of wish magic."

"So, we can use it to wish for something?" Storm said.

"Yes," the Tricorn told him. "You should be very honored the mother dragon gave you such a gift. But use it well. Each scale will only grant a single wish."

Willow looked around at her friends. "What are we going to wish for?"

"We should decide together," said Troy. "As a team."

"We'll have to think about it very carefully," said Sapphire.

Storm nodded.

"Go and think about it," the Tricorn told them.

Storm took the scale, and he and the others walked away from the platform. "What should we wish for?" Storm said, putting the scale down on the snow.

"I don't know," said Willow.

"New bags for us all?" said Sapphire.

"New stable blankets?" suggested Troy.

"A feast," said Storm.

"How about some shamrock, since we didn't win the treasure hunt?" Willow suggested.

They looked at each other.

"All those wishes would be good, but somehow they don't seem special enough," said Sapphire slowly.

Willow knew exactly what Sapphire meant.

Just then they heard the sound of disappointed whinnies behind them. They swung around. Oriel and his team were standing by the wooden crates of shamrock.

"The shamrock's ruined!" Willow heard Oriel exclaim. She wondered what he meant.

Atlas trotted over with Sirona. "The lids on the crates weren't closed tightly enough," he said. "Shamrock goes bad in cold weather, and it's been out here all day with the frost getting to it."

Oriel and his friends looked really upset.

"Don't worry," Atlas told them. "You might not be able to have a term's supply of shamrock for winning, but we'll find you another prize. A trophy or a medal or something."

Oriel bit his lip. "Okay," he said slowly.

Willow felt very sorry for him and his friends. A trophy or a medal was nice but nowhere near as amazing as a term's supply of shamrock. An idea exploded into her brain. She swung around quickly to the others. "I've got it! I know what we can wish for!"

"What?" Troy asked.

Willow beamed. "A term's supply of shamrock — *for the whole school!*"

The others gasped.

"That's a brilliant idea!" whinnied Storm.

"Just perfect!" said Sapphire.

"Come on, let's tell the Tricorn!" Troy exclaimed.

Ten minutes later, all the unicorns — teachers and students — were standing around the wooden table munching delightedly on big piles of delicious shamrock.

Willow sighed in contentment. There were lots more crates of shamrock kept safely in one of the feed stores, enough shamrock for everyone to have some every day for the rest of the term. The Tricorn had been delighted by their wish.

"I can see the dragon made a wise choice when she gave you a wishing scale," he said. "I'm very proud of you all."

The words echoed in Willow's head. She felt as if she were glowing. She and her friends might not have won the treasure hunt that day, but it didn't matter. They'd had a great adventure, helped Littleclaw, and made everyone in the school really happy. What could be better?

Troy nudged her. "It's been a good day, hasn't it?"

"It's been fantastic!" Willow looked at him and smiled.